TEARS OF TERROR

A NOVELLA BY

ALANA TERRY

ONE

CHELSEA KNEW from the moment she stepped onto the airplane that she was in over her head.

Imposter syndrome. That's what her life coach called this feeling. The sense that no matter how far Chelsea advanced in her field, she still lived each and every day in constant fear of being discovered.

What would her colleagues do when they realized she was a fraud?

Chelsea had begged and schmoozed and pleaded in order to get this assignment. And now that she was on her way to Detroit, the nerves threatened to make her throw up.

Great. That's all she needed to start her three-hour flight.

Chelsea was one of the first passengers to board. A few men in stuffy business suits glared at her first-class seat, no doubt wondering why a 23-year-old who barely topped five feet tall needed that much extra leg room.

The truth was Chelsea didn't need the extra leg room. She'd splurged for the upgrade because her life coach told her to. If Chelsea wanted other people to take her and her career seriously, she had to take herself and her career seriously.

Starting with first-class seats.

She shouldn't feel guilty, right? After all, it was Clark's idea, not hers. She was just doing what her life coach told her to do.

Now that she was sitting here, with twice the space she actually needed, Chelsea couldn't remember why this frivolous luxury had seemed like such a good idea.

Tired of questioning herself, her career choices, and her right to be sitting here in first class, Chelsea did her best to silence that inner critic she hated so much. Instead, she did what came most naturally to her as a writer. She stared at the travelers as they boarded the plane, trying to come up with backstories for each and every one of them.

There were two girls, college aged by the looks of them, giggling as they lugged their mismatched carry-ons down the aisle. "You're gonna love Alaska," said one with bright blue highlights in her hair. "It's wicked awesome."

Alaska. Chelsea tried to picture what that might be like, but all her mind could conjure up were images of sled dogs and igloos. Somehow, she doubted that's how this cosmopolitan young passenger lived.

A scowling man with an SVSU sweatshirt boarded soon after. Chelsea thought through all of the local colleges and universities in the Boston area, trying to figure out if she could place the acronym. He wasn't dressed like a typical businessman. Maybe a divorcé on the way to visit his kids? He didn't strike Chelsea as the type to be racing off toward an illicit affair. More likely he was flying to Detroit to visit his beloved granny.

Chelsea sat back in her seat, ignoring the initial pangs of what was likely to turn into a piercing headache. When she'd graduated with her journalism degree, Chelsea had been so excited. So eager. A stereotype, really. Journalism major about to make a name for herself while simultaneously changing the world one perfectly constructed para-graph at a time.

And here she was, just a few years later, already turning into another trope — the jaded, lonely single woman wondering what she was doing chasing scoops and investi-gating scandals when the very next week the public would forget everything she wrote about in the first place.

Chelsea had begged her editor for the chance to cover the Brown Elementary con-troversy. A primary school in Detroit had been built on land that had once been the illegal dumping grounds for a pharmaceu-tical company. Tiny kindergartners were landing in the ER with respiratory problems and horrific fevers and rashes, but the school district claimed it had nothing to do with the school's location. Chelsea didn't understand why the entire country hadn't already shown up to march on the superintendent's home. Most people on the East Coast hadn't even heard of Brown Elementary School.

It was the kind of story that propelled Chelsea into reporting in the first place. Im-migrant parents, many who could barely speak English, weren't given a voice. The children served by Brown Elementary were among Detroit's poorest, which is why the superintendent assumed he could get away with poisoning each and every one of them.

At her most zealous, Chelsea would have considered this the perfect assignment. Brown Elementary was news on a national scale. It was also the entire reason she dove into journalism as a wide-eyed first-year college student in the first place. To give a voice to the voiceless. To speak up for the downtrodden, shine the light on oppression, and just about any other cliché you could come up with.

But now she knew what to expect. She'd show up in Detroit, interview some of the parents whose kids had fallen ill, talk to the few key players who were trying to stand up for this underrepresented community. Then she'd fly back to Boston, type up her story, maybe even get choked up as she did her best to represent the frustration these parents felt. If she did her job well, she might even get a little nod from her editor, a pat on the back or a "Nice article" from one of her colleagues.

And then nothing.

No marches on Detroit. No public outcry. No real justice for the kids of Brown Elementary.

In short, no change.

So why did she keep doing it?

At her most jaded, she'd probably answer because it paid the bills. A journalism degree wasn't cheap, and at the rate she was going she'd have to keep writing until she was eighty to pay off all her debt.

But there was still something inside her, something that hadn't yet been completely hardened. The idealistic, trusting, impossible hope that this time would be different. Her upcoming article would be the one that made that lasting impact. That effected positive change. That united citizens from across the political spectrum, that inspired the general public to rise up and support the children of Detroit.

She could always hope, right?

Chelsea opened the lid of her water bottle and took a big drink.

Working on this story was a dream come true for her, and she didn't want to reach such a pessimistic state that she refused to see it for the incredible opportunity it was.

As men, women, and children continued

to file past her first-class seat, Chelsea took a deep breath, reminded herself that this trip represented the entire reason she'd gotten into journalism in the first place, and allowed her mind to hope and dream.

TWO

FLIGHTS COMING into Boston had been delayed due to weather, and Chelsea's plane was late to take off. They should be in the air by now, but they hadn't even shut the doors.

Chelsea had spent the past twenty minutes watching more and more passengers board, trying to dream up life stories for each and every one of them.

There was a Middle Eastern man traveling with his aged father. A man in a Hawaiian shirt, followed by a surly looking teen. Moms with babies, parents traveling with toddlers. A woman boarded whom Chelsea recognized as a well-known Bible study teacher. Chelsea's mom had been reading Meredith Crowley's books and watching her videos for over a decade. It had been a few years since Chelsea had regularly attended church with her parents, but every so often her mom would send her a link to one of Meredith Crowley's podcast episodes. Chelsea was surprised when Meredith continued past the first-class seats and headed toward economy.

An eccentric old woman with shockingly white hair boarded. She was even shorter than Chelsea, but there was something fiery in the old woman's face. Chelsea tried to think up an appropriate backstory. A doctor? Teacher? Maybe a flight nurse. There was something confident, something piercing in the woman's expression. It reminded Chelsea of an interview she'd done a few months ago with an old woman who had the distinction of being the very first female detective on Boston's police force. Whoever this passenger on the airplane was, Chelsea could sense she had the spirit of an adventurer. A pioneer.

Chelsea liked to think of herself in the same way. At least at one point she had. Female journalists weren't oddities anymore, but there were still obvious roadblocks she faced on her way to success. Any time one of the men she was sent to interview called her "Sweetie," any time a colleague or a lead tried to flirt with her, Chelsea was reminded of the inherent setbacks of her position. Unfortunately the environment was hostile enough that women were suspicious and jealous of each other instead of joining forces and standing up for themselves. Chelsea knew for a fact that some of her colleagues talked behind her back, complaining and gossiping that the only reason she'd progressed as far as she had in her career was because she was a pretty face. As hard as Chelsea tried to keep her reputation squeaky clean and her work relationships free from drama, there were still people who thought she was advancing in her career by sleeping with her bosses.

As if.

Chelsea's coach told her that the only way to prove these gossips wrong was to become an even better journalist. The problem with Clark's advice was that with each new step Chelsea took up the ladder of acclaim, there were over a dozen of her colleagues who hated Chelsea for her advancement and made up horrible lies about her success.

Chelsea was storing up all these experiences. One day she planned to write a memoir exposing the rampant sexism and harassment female journalists still faced in the twenty-first century. Until then, she had to do exactly what Clark told her to do in those coaching calls she was paying so much for. Focus on advancing her career, silencing the inner voice that told her she wasn't making any difference.

"Ladies and gentlemen, I'm Tracy, one of your flight attendants today." The voice pulled Chelsea out of her pity party. While the flight attendant recited her safety speech, Chelsea sat back in her seat and tried to relax. She'd been working insanely long hours, preparing for her Detroit trip, finishing up work on a story about police brutality in a city as purportedly progressive and forward-thinking as Boston. If anything, Chelsea deserved a few hours of uninterrupted rest. She'd already made herself a promise that on the way to Detroit she wouldn't pull out any writing. Her cell was prepped with dozens of podcast episodes she'd been meaning to catch up on. Nothing overtly work related. Mostly true crime shows she liked to follow. And if she felt guilty being that frivolous with her time, she had several workbook assignments due to Clark before their coaching call next week.

"The captain has closed the doors," Tracy announced to the cabin, "and we'll be taking off shortly. Welcome aboard Flight 219, offering you nonstop service to Detroit."

THREE

WHILE THE PASSENGER seated beside her slept, Chelsea pulled out the workbook assignments Clark had emailed her last week. Typically, she wouldn't want to write anything so personal with strangers looking over her shoulder, but her neighbor was dead to the world, the aisle was twice as wide as the ones in coach, so Chelsea had all the privacy she could want.

She'd met Clark last year, covering a story about the digital nomad lifestyle. Clark was based in Boston, but he'd set up his online coaching practice so he could travel the world. After their interview, she'd been intrigued by him and the raving testimonials of his clients, so she signed up for an initial coaching consult. She'd been his student for only about six months, and already Clark had called her for their coaching sessions from too many different exotic locations for Chelsea to remember.

There were aspects of the nomadic lifestyle Chelsea found alluring. Like never having to live in an area with snow if she didn't want to. Last month, Clark had set up his laptop in a little coworking space in New Zealand. He said he would have liked to stay there longer, but the time difference made it difficult for him to connect with his clients on the East Coast. Now, if Chelsea remembered correctly, he was temporarily settled in Costa Rica, in a little village where the average temperatures never dipped below 65 or above 72.

Yes, that was something Chelsea could definitely get used to.

Still, she wondered if Clark ever got lonely. Chelsea had been born and raised in Worcester. Her parents and grandparents and she all lived within five miles of each other. Her older brother was the odd one out, having settled with his new wife in Delaware, which may as well have been the deep south as far as the rest of the family was concerned.

Chelsea's family was close, relationally and not just geographically. She ate dinner with her parents at least once a week, more often than that when her apartment's hot water heater acted up or the coin-op washing machines downstairs stopped working. She'd specifically planned her trip to Detroit so that she could have her article researched, written, and on her editor's desk with time to spare before Christmas.

Chelsea stared at her notebook page, thinking about her schedule for the next few days. The Detroit superintendent was impossible to reach by phone, but that didn't mean Chelsea wouldn't try to get a quote from him in person. She had an interview lined up with a medical doctor who'd treated some of the elementary students who'd fallen ill. In two days, a group of parents were meeting at a local YMCA to discuss the situation.

Chelsea tapped her pen on her tray table, reminding herself she wasn't supposed to be thinking about work right now. That's something she and Clark had talked about extensively in their coaching calls. Chelsea needed to develop better boundaries to ensure that her entire life didn't get overrun by journalism. So far, she hadn't found too much success in that nebulous quest for work-life balance. She'd joined a gym but stopped going after that creepy janitor kept ogling her during spin class. She went online a week later and read that two years ago another employee had been fired and faced legal charges for hiding in a closet in the women's locker room. Next time, Chelsea wouldn't join a gym without reading the reviews first. Except now she was locked into a year-long contract.

Well, nobody could claim she hadn't tried.

Chelsea's best friend from high school was working as a youth leader at a large church in the Cambridge area. It was the perfect job for Brie, really. Even as teens, Brie had been the most serious about her faith, and Chelsea was happy her friend had found a calling that was not only rewarding but offered her a regular paycheck.

It seemed as if everyone Chelsea knew when she was younger was now settled into real life. Brie had church. Her brother had his wife and new job out in Delaware, as well as something like a dozen nieces and nephews he saw on an almost daily basis.

Chelsea knew she should be thankful for her job and the opportunities God had given her. Heaven knew finding steady work as a journalist straight out of college was on the same level as stumbling across a winning lottery ticket while picking up litter in a parking lot. So why did she feel like she was still searching for her life's meaning?

Clark told her it was a normal stage of young adulthood. Brie said it was because Chelsea still hadn't surrendered her life totally over to God, whatever that meant.

Mom thought this sense of unrest came because Chelsea had such miserable luck in the dating world.

Whatever the reason, Chelsea couldn't shake the feeling that something was missing from her life, and that unease only made her feel guilty. She had every reason to be thankful. Her sense of dissatisfaction with her personal status quo was the reason she'd hired Clark to be her life coach in the first place. That and the fact that when she interviewed him, he seemed to light up every time he talked about helping people discover their life's deeper meaning. Well, if he could help

Chelsea find even a tenth of the motivation and passion she saw in him, he was well worth his monthly retainer.

That was why she was so disciplined about completing each and every task he assigned her. That was why she'd printed up these dozen workbook pages and was committed to knocking some of them out before she put in her ear buds and tuned out the world with something light and funny to listen to.

She took a deep breath, tried to get her mind into a state of gentle awareness like Clark taught her, and began the process of filling out her first worksheet.

The problem with Clark's coaching method was that Chelsea still hadn't learned to turn off her inner editor. She read each and every word of her answer through Clark's eyes, wondering what he'd think of her, what he'd say to her.

Sometimes, hearing his gentle encouragement in the back of her head was immensely helpful. Like the time she wrote about how stupid she felt for stumbling over her words at a meeting with mostly male colleagues. *I hate it when I make myself sound like a fool,* she'd written, and immediately heard Clark's encouraging words.

Would you tell a five-year-old that she was stupid and you hated her if she pronounced a word wrong or got a little flustered with public speaking?

No, of course she wouldn't.

This coaching process was taking longer than Chelsea hoped, but at least she was learning how to be gentle with herself.

Chelsea's mom didn't approve. According to her, it wasn't right for a female to get counseling from a male. It also didn't help that Mom didn't understand the difference between a life coach and a licensed therapist to begin with. She assumed that the fact that Chelsea was talking to anybody about her deep personal issues meant she was somehow psychologically scarred.

"I didn't think we did that bad of a job raising you," she'd say, as if all Chelsea and Clark talked about were the lowest points in Chelsea's childhood.

Brie was a better listener, but even though she never said so, Chelsea got the sense that her best friend would approve more if Chelsea went to a pastor or Christian counselor.

Chelsea wasn't against church or Christianity. She still attended services with her parents if she was home for the weekend, and she couldn't remember missing an Easter sunrise or Christmas Eve service in her entire life. Sometimes it bothered her the way Christians she loved acted as though she was selfish or somehow less of a believer because she wasn't working for the church like Brie or attending Bible studies or prayer meetings three or four days a week like her mom. Chelsea loved the Lord but had other interests and hobbies outside of church. What was so wrong with that?

The worksheet she'd been journaling on had questions about her past achievements. When Chelsea saw all the accomplishments she'd made in the past two years written out on paper, she felt even more guilty for being so dissatisfied. If Chelsea could have seen this list during her first year of college, if she could have known where all that hard work would one day take her, she probably would have started squealing with giddy excitement.

So where was the joy, the spark?

Clark's worksheet — his ta-da list as opposed to a to-do list — was meant to help Chelsea realize all that she did have to be thankful for, but instead it just reinforced her fear that there was something intrinsically wrong with her.

Imagine you're receiving an award for all the hard work you've done. Your friends, loved ones, and colleagues are all there cheering for you. How do you feel?

Chelsea stared at the question, wondering if she'd answer it truthfully or the way Clark expected.

She poised her pen above the lines. *Honestly*, she wrote, *I'd feel like a total fraud. Like any minute whoever gave me the award would turn on the lights and stop the applause halfway through and tell everyone that it was all some giant mistake.*

She let out her breath. Her answer wasn't going to make her life coach happy.

Is that what you'd tell a little five-year-old girl if she was about to accept an award she'd earned by her hard work? Clark's voice in her mind was gentle but firm.

Of course she wouldn't tell that to a proud little kid on the happiest day of her life. So why did she say it to herself? What was wrong with her?

Maybe Clark gave her these assignments to prove how messed up she was. Maybe it was all some giant ploy so she'd keep on paying him for coaching.

Chelsea's negative thoughts were interrupted when a passenger tapped her on the shoulder. It was the same white-haired woman Chelsea had been studying during the boarding process.

"Excuse me," the old woman said, her wrinkles breaking out into tiny streams when she smiled.

Chelsea shut her notebook so the old woman couldn't read what she'd written.

"The bathroom in the back of the plane is full," the traveler explained, "so I came up here to use this one. As soon as I saw you here, I knew I had to stop and say something. I don't usually do this type of thing, but I just had to introduce myself."

She reached out a hand, which Chelsea took automatically.

"My name is Lucy Jean," the passenger said, "but I insist on being called Grandma Lucy. And I believe the Lord has a message for you."

FOUR

CHELSEA BLINKED up at the stranger. A message from God? It sounded like something her mom would arrange. Hire some weirdo on Craigslist to stalk Chelsea on her flight and make small talk about Jesus, remind Chelsea that there were about a million ways she could become a better Christian if she just set her mind to it.

Chelsea stared and didn't know what to say.

Despite her obvious age, Grandma Lucy showed no signs of pain or stiffness when she squatted down in the aisle to bring herself to Chelsea's eye level.

"I wasn't supposed to be on this flight," she began. "But the airlines changed my itinerary, and wouldn't you know it, I told the Lord that if he wanted to disrupt my plans, he's more than welcome to. I figure that if he put me on a different flight, it's because there's someone on this plane who needs to hear about his love."

Chelsea realized that she'd rather fill out a hundred of Clark's journaling pages, no matter how bad they made her feel about herself, than sit here and get preached at. Both her mom and best friend wanted Chelsea to take her faith more seriously, but they certainly wouldn't start lecturing her in the aisle on an airplane full of strangers.

"I think the bathroom looks unoccupied," Chelsea said in a quiet voice. Too quiet.

Grandma Lucy didn't even appear to have heard.

"There's something I sensed in my spirit the moment I saw you," she went on. "God has called you to something amazing and profound. Tell me, do you have children?"

Of course this fanatic woman would assume that the only way Chelsea could make God happy was to pop out a bunch of kids. "No," she answered.

Grandma Lucy didn't look surprised.

"Well then, tell me what you do for a living. Are you a teacher, maybe?"

"No, a journalist."

The old woman's eyes lit up. "Journalist? My grandson is a journalist. Have you read anything by Ian McCallister?"

"The name sounds familiar," Chelsea answered.

"Well, let me tell you, the world needs more Christian journalists, that's for sure. With all the terrible things going on today, every reporter with a slanted agenda …" Her voice trailed off, and Chelsea dared hope it meant she'd run out of things to say, but apparently that wasn't the case.

"I just want to tell you that I think it's amazing, the work that you're doing."

Chelsea stared at the stranger in surprise. What did this little old lady know about her work? She hadn't even given Grandma Lucy her name.

Before Chelsea could do or say anything in protest, Grandma Lucy grabbed Chelsea's hand, seized it in hers, and started to pray.

"Dear Lord, great and merciful Savior, you are so good to us, and you are so gracious to look past our shortcomings and use us for your kingdom as you see fit. I pray for my dear sister today, Lord. I believe that you've anointed this young woman. I believe you have unbelievable plans for her, plans to prosper her and not to harm her. I believe that you will walk with her through whatever trials she might have to face, and that you will use these storms in her life to draw her closer to you. Teach her to rely on you, Lord. Teach her that without you, she can do absolutely nothing. Teach her that you are the way and the truth and the life, and that it is such a wonderous and glorious honor to be able to worship you as our Lord and Savior.

"May you guide her in every step she takes. Keep her as the apple of your eye. I believe you've poured out on her an incredible gift, a gift that she wants to use for you and for your glory."

Grandma Lucy's eyes were open and staring overtly at her notebook. Chelsea was glad she'd thought to close it before this strange encounter.

She was trying to form the words to explain that the old woman's actions were making her uncomfortable when Grandma Lucy stood up, straightened her blouse, and let go of Chelsea's hand. "Well then," she said, as if they'd been chatting about something as innocuous as the weather, "it looks like the bathroom's open now. We'll talk more later."

And she walked down the aisle, leaving Chelsea's brain reeling.

FIVE

AN HOUR after her encounter with the outspoken stranger, Chelsea still hadn't been able to shake off the old woman's words. What did it all mean? Pieces and fragments of Grandma Lucy's prayer floated chaotically through her brain.

I believe that you will walk with her through whatever trials she might have to face, and that you will use these storms in her life to draw her closer to you. In a way, Chelsea knew that these words were meant to somehow encourage and inspire her, but they sounded more ominous than anything else. Was this eccentric old lady seriously wishing bad things to happen in Chelsea's life just so she could get right with the Lord again?

What kind of sense did that make?

Teach her that without you, she can do absolutely nothing. Chelsea thought about her list of accomplishments, what Clark called her ta-da list. Well, that was something, wasn't it? In addition to feeling guilty for not appreciating her life more than she did, was Chelsea supposed to do penance because she hadn't acknowledged God enough for all that she'd achieved?

Teach her that you are the way and the truth and the life, and that it is such a wonderous and glorious honor to be able to worship you as our Lord and Savior. Never had a prayer sounded so preachy to Chelsea's ears. Never had she felt so condemned, so unworthy.

Clark would tell her she was giving this stranger too much authority. Nobody could make Chelsea feel sad or glad or guilty but herself. This stranger had no bearing on Chelsea's life. Her words shouldn't matter.

And yet somehow they did.

Such a wonderous and glorious honor to be able to worship you as our Lord and Savior ... That last part of Grandma Lucy's prayer stuck out the most. When had Chelsea ever thought of worshiping God as a privilege or honor? Church was something she attended to keep her mom placated. God and the Bible were things Chelsea talked about with her best friend because faith was important to Brie, just like journalism and politics were important to Chelsea.

Such a wonderous and glorious honor ... Was it possible that this was the thing that had been missing from Chelsea's life? Was that why she'd felt so dissatisfied for so long?

She tried to imagine what Clark would tell her if he were sitting next to her, if they could talk about this bizarre encounter with a stranger on the plane.

"She didn't even ask if I wanted her to pray for me," Chelsea would whine.

"And how did that make you feel?" he would prompt.

How did it make her feel? She knew how it should make her feel.

That part was easy.

It should make her feel completely annoyed. Grandma Lucy didn't even know if Chelsea was a Christian. What if she was a Muslim or a Jew and found Grandma Lucy's prayer to Jesus totally offensive?

What if Chelsea was just an introverted and somewhat shy young woman who didn't appreciate having that much attention drawn to herself? Who wanted a stranger prying into her personal life like that?

Chelsea should be annoyed. Put off. It'd be well within her rights to complain to the flight attendant, force them to tell Grandma Lucy not to bother her anymore. Maybe she'd even write a blog post about her experience. Something that could serve as a warning to other religious fanatics to be careful not to shove their beliefs down people's throats on an airplane, where it was literally impossible to get up and leave to end an awkward conversation.

But Chelsea didn't feel annoyed. She didn't feel put off.

Something had happened to her during the old woman's prayer, something that made her wish for a quiet place to sit and think. Think and maybe cry.

There was no mistaking that Grandma Lucy had been out of place. You can't just walk up to a stranger and ignore all semblance of personal space and privacy. That's not how life works. Not how a civilized society works.

And yet ...

Lord, I believe that you've anointed this young woman. Anointed. It was a word Chelsea had heard. A word she could define. But what was this strange old woman trying to say to her? Chelsea was anointed ... What did that even mean?

I believe you have unbelievable plans for her, plans to prosper her and not to harm her. One of Chelsea's biggest frustrations with herself was that she had no spark of joy when she thought about the future. Sure, she planned on advancing in her career. She planned on covering bigger, more impressive stories. More bylines. Better job offers. Bigger benefit packages.

But what for?

Plans to prosper her and not to harm her ... Chelsea tried to imagine the future that this old woman was envisioning. Was it possible that Chelsea's destiny included more than growing a name for herself, working her fingers raw at her laptop, and giving herself eyestrain and migraine headaches from staring at her screen for ten hours a day?

Of course there was something more to life. Isn't that why Chelsea had hired Clark in the first place? It wasn't like she wasn't trying to better herself, improve her outlook. Carve out that glorious future Grandma Lucy seemed to believe was in store for her.

And yet here she was, still filling out the same workbook pages, still asking herself the same questions. Had she and Clark made any real progress at all since they'd met?

Teach her to rely on you, Lord ... Guide her in every step she takes. The way Grandma Lucy talked about it, you would think that Chelsea could jump online and schedule an appointment with the Almighty himself just like she did when she needed to talk to her life coach. Wouldn't that make things simpler? Not to mention the fact that she wouldn't have to pay God for his time.

But life didn't work like that. God gave people the Bible. He gave people consciences. He gave people good teachers. And the rest was up to them to figure out, right?

Or maybe there was something more to it. Chelsea didn't know exactly what the Lord was trying to tell her right now, but she desperately wanted to find out.

SIX

THE PLANE HIT a patch of turbulence, and Chelsea realized she'd been staring at Clark's worksheet page but hadn't written anything since her unexpected conversation with Grandma Lucy. Even now the old woman's words from her prayer still rang in Chelsea's ears. A siren song. Calling her somewhere.

But where?

It was impossible to give a name to the ennui, the unrest. All Chelsea knew was that she wanted to figure out what her soul was trying to tell her. She needed something more out of life. She'd known that for years. That was why she hired a life coach in the first place.

But there was something else. Something

still missing after all these months of intense journaling and dozens of hours of reflection. Her mom would say that what Chelsea was missing was an intimate connection with the Lord. Even Brie, who wasn't nearly as tactless as her mother could be, felt the same way.

But Chelsea was scared. She'd met too many obnoxious Christians. Heard too many horrible stories from her colleagues about the bigotry and chauvinism and hatred that infected the church.

Chelsea didn't want to be like that. Didn't want to breathe Bible verses down people's necks like her mom. Didn't want to devote her life to church ministry like Brie. More than anything, Chelsea didn't want to turn into the kind of Christian who'd make a scene of herself on a crowded airplane to kneel down in the aisle and pray for a complete stranger.

She wanted to be herself. Chelsea. The journalist. The writer. The career woman.

She just wanted to be a happier version of herself.

Was that so much to ask?

For a couple years now, Chelsea had wondered if what she was really dealing with was some sort of clinical depression. It had gotten to the point last winter that if she hadn't been worried about insurance coverage, she probably would have made an appointment to talk to her family doctor. She hadn't brought it up to her parents. Thankfully, she was still managing just fine, but maybe all the mental unrest she was experiencing was nothing more than a chemical unbalance. How could she really know unless she talked about it with an expert, right?

Chelsea squeezed her eyes shut. She was tired of being so mopey, so down all the time. She had a great life. Hadn't that ta-da list she wrote for Clark proved that? Chelsea deserved to be happy. Deserved a brain that could truly experience a deep sense of appreciation for all that she'd accomplished.

Maybe once she got back from Detroit she'd call the doctor …

"Help!" The desperate scream from several rows behind her made Chelsea jump in her seat. She bumped her thigh on the tray, hurtling her notebook to the ground, as a young woman struggled in the aisle with a middle-aged man in a Hawaiian shirt.

"Help me!" the girl screamed again.

A flight attendant raced ahead. Chelsea

didn't know if she was supposed to stare or join the screaming or simply mind her own business.

She overheard someone shout the word *kidnapped*, and her heart froze for an instant. What was going on?

"Let her go." There were several passengers in the aisle now, and everyone was trying to pry a teenaged girl away from the man in the Hawaiian shirt. Chelsea didn't feel right staring, but what choice did she have? One of her colleagues had recently written an article about human trafficking in the US and how airlines were now training all their personnel to spot potential victims. Is that what was going on?

A muscular man planted himself squarely in the aisle. "Air marshal," he announced authoritatively, pulling out his sidearm. "Freeze."

For a moment, Chelsea allowed herself to experience relief. If there was an air marshal on board, everything would be under control. This girl would be saved. Her assailant would get the full punishment allowed under federal law. Life would go on as normal. Chelsea was already thinking about a pitch for a new story about air marshals, airline safety, and human trafficking.

The captain's voice sounded over the PA, but before he could get out a complete sentence, his announcement was cut short by the screams of another terrified passenger. Chelsea instinctively jerked her body around to see what was happening behind her. Two men were now attacking the air marshal. One of them grabbed the officer's gun. This time it was Chelsea who screamed as the man brought the butt of the gun down on the air marshal's skull. He crumpled to the ground and lay in a grotesque heap in the aisle.

A man Chelsea hadn't noticed before raised the air marshal's gun above his head. "I'm in charge of this airplane now," he declared. "My name is Bradley Strong, and I suggest you all do exactly as I say."

SEVEN

CHELSEA'S HEART couldn't handle the stress. Any instant, it was going to give out entirely.

Her head was light. Was she even breathing?

"Listen up," Bradley bellowed. His voice carried and echoed through every crevice and cranny of the cabin. "Let me tell you how it's gonna go."

Behind him, the man in the Hawaiian shirt was binding the air marshal and dragging his unconscious body to the back of the cabin. Chelsea thought she saw him make eye contact and give a silent nod to another passenger as well. How many men were in on this plot to take over their plane?

"You have to let us go," a woman pleaded. "Please, you don't want to do this."

"No." Bradley's voice was level and eerily controlled. He continued to aim the air marshal's gun overhead. "The truth is I don't want to do this, but the Detroit mayor and his crony superintendent have failed our kids. All year, we've been complaining about the health hazards of the Brown Elementary School playground. All year, we've been calling, petitioning, and demanding that the superintendent move our children to a safer location. And you know what? Nobody's listened. Until now."

Chelsea's brain was struggling to keep up with his rant. It didn't make sense. What did any of these passengers on board have to do with Brown Elementary School or the Detroit school system?

Another pocket of turbulence shook the cabin. Several passengers screamed. Chelsea was so shocked she couldn't even be certain if she'd been one of them, but the raw soreness of her throat suggested she was.

A man from the back of the cabin took advantage of the chaos and raced at Bradley. While the plane jerked yet again, the two men grappled, grunting loudly. Chelsea was about to be sick, maybe from the fear or the turbulence. Maybe both.

A single shot rang out. Everything happened so quickly, Chelsea didn't even realize it was the gun that had fired until she saw the man who attacked Bradley lying in the aisle, a pool of blood forming around him.

Bradley used his foot to push the man to the side, stepped over his body, and addressed the passengers in an eerie monotone.

"Anybody else feel like questioning my authority?"

Chelsea didn't know what to say or what to do. It was one thing to be a bystander on a flight where a kidnapped girl was rescued from her abductor. Her brain still hadn't processed that event, and now she was supposed to take in the fact that she was on a hijacked plane, the terrorist had a gun, and one passenger had been shot. She wasn't sure if the air marshal had survived his attack or not, but he was now bound in the back of the cabin. Even if he wasn't tied up and unconscious, what could he do now to help them?

The man in the aisle was most definitely dead, however. Chelsea could tell.

When she was a little girl, Chelsea and

her parents once stumbled across the scene of an accident. A drunk man had smashed his car straight into a telephone pole on a deserted stretch of road in the middle of the day.

He was still alive when her family pulled up to see if they could offer any help.

"Don't get out of the car," Dad ordered. "And keep your eyes shut no matter what."

Of course, that kind of rule was next to impossible for an inquisitive seven-year-old to follow. Chelsea had stared, her eyes both wide and dry, as her dad pulled the man out of the car and her mom attempted CPR. The entire scene lasted only a few minutes, and her parents insisted the man didn't die until he was en route to the hospital, but Chelsea knew what she saw. Knew that the life had already left him.

And she immediately understood why her parents had ordered her not to look.

Chelsea mentioned the story to Clark as an aside one day. He wanted to explore the possibility that the helplessness and hopelessness Chelsea experienced as a little girl, forced to stay in her parents' car while a man literally died in front of her eyes, sparked the passion she now had to speak up for the downtrodden, to use her words to give voice to the voiceless.

She had never thought about the incident in those terms before, but his hypothesis seemed logical.

Since then, Chelsea had been to one funeral wake and avoided looking at the body. Until now, she'd never seen another dead person.

Until now ...

The hijacker had ordered the passengers to take out their cell phones and record his tirade.

"My name is Bradley Strong," he repeated to the cameras. "I reside at 324 Trenton Street in Detroit, Michigan. My children attend Brown Elementary School. If you've been paying attention to the news at all, you'll know what that means."

Chelsea's heart was pounding all the way up in her throat, not just because she was on a plane with a murderous terrorist and at least one dead body already, but also because she was so familiar with the controversy at the school Bradley was talking about. For a sickening moment, she feared he must know. Must know that she was a journalist covering the story. Maybe he'd blame her and people like her for not exposing the situation earlier. Plans for the building started over a year ago. Now here it was nearly Christmas, and the poor kids had been attending classes on this toxic wasteland since the fall.

Chelsea understood his frustration. If she had children of her own, she'd rather move to a different state than send them to a place like Brown. Unfortunately, the families served by that school generally lacked the funds to move even to a different neighborhood. The town hall meetings where they could have voiced their complaints were held during working hours when most of them were on the clock, and a significant portion of them didn't feel comfortable communicating in English, which is how their children's school ended up being built on a former pharmaceutical sludge pile in the first place.

Chelsea had never experienced anything like what the families at Brown Elementary had, at least not firsthand. Growing up in Worcester, she'd been smack dab in the center of middle class. Comfortable suburbs. Involved parents. Quiet cul de sac. Sometimes she felt guilty. What right did she have trying to speak up for the oppressed when her entire life had been so comfortable?

Clark told her that instead of resenting her privileged existence, she should leverage her position as a relatively attractive, reasonably articulate white female college graduate in order to raise awareness for those who were more easily overlooked. His words even coincided with a Bible verse Brie liked to quote: *From everyone who has been given much, much will be demanded; and from the one who has been entrusted with much, much more will be asked.*

Chelsea sometimes wondered why matters of faith came so much simpler to her friend. Brie had grown up with an alcoholic father and an enabling mother. Her older brother had been in and out of jail on multiple drug charges, and her family had always struggled to make ends meet. Even now, Brie was living in a studio apartment in a neighborhood rough enough that Chelsea begged her to get a smart security system, or at least a second deadbolt for the door that she could fasten from the inside.

As a minority, as a young adult from a not-so-idyllic family background, Brie had every reason to be anxious, depressed, and maladjusted. But she was the most put-together person Chelsea knew, which only made Chelsea feel even more guilty for the personal struggles she'd been wrestling with since her early teens.

Bradley continued his tirade against the state of Michigan, the Detroit mayor, the nation who sat back and did nothing while helpless children were being poisoned day in and day out. The majority of his rant was directed at the superintendent of the Detroit school district.

"Charles Weston has failed our kids," he spat out. It was a name Chelsea was quite familiar with. In her preliminary research on the Brown scandal, Charles Weston stood out as the primary culprit, which was why she'd been working so hard to try to get a hold of him before she'd made this trip.

The fact that the terrorist holding her plane hostage was protesting the very story Chelsea was flying out to Detroit to cover was unnerving. It was bad enough sitting here with an armed gunman who'd already killed at least one passenger. But the fact that she and Bradley were somehow both concerned about the same travesty impacting the kids of Detroit made her feel squeamish and alarmed. Airplane hijackers were supposed to be greedy, monstrous villains. Was it possible that Bradley was nothing more than a desperate father, doing anything and everything in his power to make it so his kids didn't get lead and arsenic poisoning when they played four-square outside after lunch?

No, that didn't make sense. Chelsea cared about the students at Brown Elementary School, which was why she was on this plane. Never in her wildest dreams would she consider hijacking one.

Maybe there was something deeper to it than this. Maybe Brown was just a smoke-screen. Maybe Bradley would have turned toward murder and terrorism no matter what school his children went to, and his frustration with the mayor of the Detroit and the school district superintendent was simply an easy excuse.

It certainly was an easier explanation to accept.

"By the way," Bradley was saying. "If Charles Weston is looking for his precious little girl, I want you to know I've been keeping Selena in good hands." He grabbed the wide-eyed teenager the air marshal had been trying to protect. Lifting her up by the collar of her T-shirt, he shoved her in front of a passenger's phone.

"Say hello to your daddy," Bradley told her, his voice taunting and full of spite.

Selena Weston was shaking so hard she could barely stand. Overcome with compassion and pity, Chelsea resisted the urge to jump out of her seat and race to the girl's side.

Just stay calm, Chelsea told herself. *Stay calm, stay quiet, and you just might get through this ordeal alive.*

EIGHT

CHELSEA HAD NEVER CONSIDERED herself
that gifted in prayer. Her mom could sit for
hours with her Bible and a cup of coffee and
pour out her heart to God while highlighting
passages of Scripture and jotting down notes
in the margins. Chelsea, on the other hand,
found her mind wandering when her dad
said grace before the evening meal.

Even now, Chelsea realized, she was no
better at praying than when she wasn't being
held hostage thirty-thousand feet above
ground by an insane murderer intent on kid-
napping, hijacking, and terrorism.

Her mind wanted to pray, but she
couldn't slow down the racing of her heart

long enough to focus on anything. There was nothing in her soul, no pleas for protection, no comforting passages of Scripture brought to mind at just the right time.

There was only uncertainty and fear.

Bradley was pacing up and down the aisle. Each and every time he came close to first class, Chelsea willed herself to grow even smaller. When his steps receded and he headed toward the back of the cabin, Chelsea experienced a surge of relief that left her head light and her body cold. A surge of relief that also left her feeling incredibly guilty, because it just meant his attentions were focused on some other helpless, terrorized passenger.

"I'm going to give Charles Weston five minutes to call me," Bradley declared. "Five minutes for a little heart-to-heart with the city's good old superintendent. We can talk about anything you like. About the elementary school you built on poison, about the grown men on the construction crew who landed in the hospital. Or maybe you'd like to talk about something else. Your daughter, maybe? I don't want to hurt her, but I assure you I will."

Chelsea couldn't bring herself to look at

the kidnapped teen who'd returned to her seat after being paraded in front of the cameras. From somewhere behind her, Chelsea heard muffled whimpering, but she had no idea if it was from Selena Weston or any of the other hundreds of passengers on the flight. They were all here, all captive. They had all seen Bradley shoot his first victim. And yet Chelsea felt incredibly alone in the horror of it, as if nobody else in the world could imagine the terror she was experiencing at this exact moment in time.

She tried to think of what Clark might tell her in a situation like this, but her coach's voice in her mind was silent.

She tried to guess what her mother would do if she were stuck here on this flight. Pray. That was probably it. Mom and Dad always talked about heaven, and they were both certain about their future in the afterlife. Chelsea believed the exact same things they did, but that didn't mean she was anywhere near ready to die.

Please, God. Chelsea couldn't think of anything else even remotely appropriate to say.

"Five minutes," Bradley repeated,

making a show of checking on the time. "Five minutes before another hostage dies."

Please, God. It was the only prayer Chelsea could muster.

She just hoped it would be enough.

NINE

BRADLEY'S TIMER BEEPED. He pulled his phone out of his pocket and turned off the alarm.

The silence was terrifying.

"That's five minutes," he declared in a monotone. "Time's up."

Chelsea held her breath. Any doubts she had about Bradley's willingness to use the air marshal's gun had already vanished when he shot the first passenger. Now it wasn't a question of whether or not he was going to kill. The only question was who would end up in the aisle next, collapsed in a puddle of blood.

For a brief stint during her tenth-grade year, Chelsea had entertained thoughts of going into the medical field. Nursing, maybe labor and delivery, she wasn't sure. Plans changed one night in youth group when they were playing a raucous game of sardines in the dark. Brie tripped over a stair on the sanctuary platform, cracking her forehead open on the baptistry. While they waited for Brie's mother to pick her up and take her to the ER, Chelsea sat beside her best friend, terrified that Brie was about to bleed to death by her side.

It was that night when Chelsea realized she could never handle blood or trauma or basically any type of emergency.

Brie was fine. She didn't even need stitches. It didn't matter how many adults and experts assured Chelsea that the amount of blood from head injuries almost always made them appear worse than they were. She'd spent ten terrible minutes convinced her best friend was going to die, just like the man in that car accident when she was a kid, and given how her body still shook the next morning when she woke up, Chelsea realized she just wasn't built to handle emergency situations.

A lot changed that night.

Brie now had a permanent scar above

her left eyebrow. The teens from youth group weren't allowed to run in the sanctuary anymore. And Chelsea gave up her plans for nursing.

Maybe if Chelsea had continued down that career path, things would be different right now. She'd have no reason to be on this flight to Detroit, for one thing.

There was a verse Chelsea and Brie had memorized when they were on the Bible quiz team together in middle school. Chelsea still remembered it verbatim: *And we know that in all things God works for the good of those who love him, who have been called according to his purpose.* It was the kind of passage meant to encourage Christians to persevere during hard times, knowing that good would eventually come from their trials.

But how would you tell that to the man Bradley had just killed?

How would you tell that to the next victim he shot?

"Mr. Weston," Bradley boomed. He spoke into the cameras that were pointed at him as if he'd hosted his own YouTube talk show for decades. Chelsea couldn't help but wonder what might have happened if he'd put this same amount of energy that he spent on hijacking this airplane into actually campaigning or raising awareness for the students of Brown Elementary.

"I've been patient with you, Mr. Weston," Bradley announced. "I've given you five minutes to call me. More than five minutes, actually. And you know what I've gotten from you? Nothing. Nada. I thought that if I made this personal, if I actually had your daughter on board this flight with me, that you'd be willing to negotiate. I guess I was wrong."

He paused, stared at the camera, and glowered. "You've had ample time," he said, "and plenty of warning. I just want you to rest assured that everything that happens from this moment forward is entirely your fault."

Chelsea turned around in her seat as Bradley's resumed pacing brought him closer to the front of the plane. She couldn't look at him, didn't dare to breathe for fear of drawing attention to herself. Was it fair? Was it right? If she made herself little, if she hoped that Bradley would pass her by, did that mean she was actively wishing for someone else to die?

She tried to picture Clark's face. Tried to

guess what her coach would tell her now to help her calm down. Help her regain her composure.

But when she pictured Clark here on this plane with her, he was just as terrified as she was.

God, help us.

There was no way over the roar of the airplane engines that Chelsea should be able to hear Bradley's boots as he stomped up and down the aisle, but her senses were heightened exponentially, and each step he took sent shivers of panic and terror racing up her spine.

"This is your fault, Mr. Weston," Bradley repeated then reached out and grabbed a flight attendant by the elbow.

"Get over here," he growled at her.

Chelsea hated herself for feeling even a hint of relief. Is this what terrorism did to you? It made you happy when somebody else was about to get killed because at least you yourself had the chance to survive. Chelsea already carried around enough guilt in her life. Guilt for not being happier, more thankful. Guilt for being depressed when she'd been blessed with such a privileged upbringing. And now she was supposed to live with survivor's guilt on top of that?

She hated herself. Hated how she'd never appreciated life until this exact moment. How sick and twisted was it that it took an act of terrorism for her to finally feel thankful for everything she'd been given?

God, I'm so sorry.

Her prayer sounded pathetic. Ridiculous. And yet she held onto what her parents and pastor and youth group leader always told her growing up. *You can be a thousand steps away from the Lord, but it's only one step back.*

She knew she was a trope. Knew she was only praying this hard because it felt as if her life literally depended on it. But that didn't change the fact that it was the sincerest offering she'd ever lifted up to heaven.

God, I'm so sorry for not taking my relationship with you more seriously. I'm so sorry that I haven't been living for you like I should. I'm so sorry for not being more thankful and loving and kind.

I'm just sorry all around.

She held her breath and waited. She'd never prayed that earnestly before in her life. Shouldn't something happen now? The air marshal should wake up, break free, and overcome the hijacker. God could send an

entire legion of angels to protect the innocent passengers. Or just strike Bradley down
dead. Didn't he do that once for one of the
wicked kings in the Old Testament?

Something.

Anything.

Instead, silence.

Silence until Bradley snarled at the trembling flight attendant, aimed his gun, and
stared at the cameras.

"Remember, Mr. Weston, this is entirely
your fault."

The shot sounded through the cabin,
ringing over the screams of the terrified passengers, then the flight attendant fell to the
floor.

Chelsea turned around in her seat so she
didn't have to watch the blood pool.

"That's another soul on Charles Weston's conscience," Bradley declared. "Five
more minutes, and if I don't hear from you
by then, another hostage dies."

TEN

CHELSEA HAD COVERED a fair number of disturbing stories in the past. A Kenyan college student attacked brutally and without provocation by a white police officer. A murdered Boston politician, a Medford pastor shot in his own home. All around Massachusetts, children went missing, spouses got beat up, victims were abused repeatedly every single day.

For most of her career, Chelsea found ways to separate herself from the trauma she covered. It was the only way she could keep on doing what she did. That didn't mean she was without compassion or empathy. It was just that because she was so compassionate and empathetic, she had to come up with coping mechanisms to protect herself from the terror and crimes she reported about on a daily basis.

Now, Chelsea wasn't even thinking about herself as a journalist. It didn't matter that her editor continued to give her bigger and more high-profile cases to cover. It didn't matter that this trip to Detroit meant Chelsea was breaking out of her local sphere and into the world of national reporting.

Who cared?

And what was it all for if Chelsea was going to be the next person to die when Bradley's timer went off anyway?

He was continuing to pace the aisles when his phone rang. He pulled it out of his pocket and answered with a smirk.

"This is Bradley." He wasn't what she would have expected a terrorist to sound like. When she looked at him, it felt as if she were staring at a man who could have been her third-grade teacher or the guy working on his laptop beside her at the corner café.

Bradley's phone was set on speaker, and Chelsea strained her ears to hear the lifeline whose voice rang out from the other side.

"This is Frank," the man said. "Brad, is that you? May I call you Brad?"

Chelsea watched as the hijacker's face and expression grew even more angry and irritated. "What do you want?" he growled. "I want to talk to the superintendent."

"I know, Brad. I know."

Chelsea tried to picture Frank on the other end of the line, tried to imagine who this man was, how he managed to get through to a cell phone on an airplane flying thirty thousand feet in the air. It wasn't until she started to get lightheaded that she realized she was holding her breath. Would this Frank person, whoever he was, manage to convince Bradley to put down his gun and let them all go?

Chelsea had never covered a real-life hostage situation before. Of course, she was familiar with the most famous cases. The Stockholm bank heist gone wrong. The Patty Hearst ordeal, where the victim ended up shocking the police and FBI by siding with her captors. Chelsea recalled details from a true-crime podcast she listened to where a rich young heiress was kidnapped, held for ransom, and ended up falling in love with her abductor.

Of course, not every hostage developed feelings of dependency on their captors. Sitting where she was, cowering in fear and drenched in sweat, Chelsea wondered how anybody could sympathize with someone like this madman in their cabin.

It certainly wasn't the first time that Chelsea had felt scared during a job. There was that riot that broke out when she was covering what should have been a peaceful prayer vigil. In another instance, Chelsea had gotten threatening letters, strongly urging her in no uncertain terms to drop a case she was covering about a senator's daughter who got kidnapped a few years ago.

In each and every one of those situations, Chelsea had been able to convince herself she wasn't in any real danger. People faced hazards at work no matter what career they chose. Chelsea's job as a journalist was tame when you compared it to the risks that firefighters and soldiers and policeman, sometimes even public schoolteachers, took each and every day.

The man on the other end of Bradley's cell phone identified himself as a hostage negotiator, but Bradley refused to talk to anybody but the Detroit superintendent. Chelsea wondered how Selena felt, the su-

perintendent's daughter who had been
kidnapped.

Chelsea had never heard of any parent
threatening anybody just because they were
unhappy with school district policies. Of
course, the scandal at Brown Elementary
and its location on toxic soil was far more
serious than whose child did or didn't make
it into honors band or whether or not high
school seniors should be allowed to drive
themselves off campus during lunch.

If her editor realized she was here on
this hijacked flight, he'd expect her to be
taking notes, documenting the terror second
by second. As Bradley got more and more
agitated, arguing with the professional negotiator, Chelsea couldn't think about work
at all.

She couldn't think about the story she
could write as a first-hand witness to
Bradley's murderous rampage. Couldn't
think about how much time and effort he
and his men must have put into planning
this takeover.

In the grips of her terror and fear,
Chelsea could hardly find the strength to
pray.

She wondered if her mom was watching

the news, if her parents had any idea what Chelsea was experiencing right here on Flight 219. Were they praying for her? Did they even know? Maybe they were just going about their normal, everyday lives, completely unaware that their daughter's plane had been hijacked. Chelsea thought about her friends. Of course, everybody at work would be seeing these events and covering them in real time, but had any of them put the puzzle pieces together to realize that one of their own was aboard this flight? What about Brie? Chelsea's best friend was notoriously bad at keeping up with current events unless she stumbled across them in her Facebook feed. Brie was probably the last person to guess what was happening on this plane.

Chelsea had lost the flow of Bradley's conversation with the hostage negotiator, but his yelling snapped her attention back to the phone call.

"You tell Weston that he calls me in two minutes," Bradley snarled, "or another hostage dies."

ELEVEN

SECONDS PASSED. Chelsea tried to mentally calculate how much time was left, but in her terror, her mind could never count past five before she lost track of where she was.

When Bradley's timer beeped, shivers of panic cascaded down Chelsea's spine, then circled around to her gut, where they sat like a monument to fear and terror.

It wasn't supposed to happen like this. She was supposed to land in Detroit in half an hour. Get off the plane, check into her room, and prepare for the next few days of interviews and investigation.

None of which she could do if she was dead.

Bradley was marching to the back of the cabin.

"Get up," he ordered.

Chelsea twisted in her seat and stared as a young woman with bright blue streaks in her hair stood up, her entire body trembling. It was the passenger from Alaska. She looked even younger than Chelsea.

This wasn't right.

But there wasn't anything Chelsea could do. Nothing but sit and stare.

"What's your name?" Bradley demanded.

"Willow," she answered.

Chelsea wanted to turn around. Wanted to shut her eyes and pretend like none of this was really happening. But she couldn't.

"Willow," Bradley repeated. His voice was disturbingly pleasant, almost charming. "Tell me something about yourself, Willow. Do you have a boyfriend?"

She gave her head a slight shake.

"Family, then? Parents?"

The young woman nodded, and a grin spread across Bradley's face.

"Is there something you'd like to say to your parents, Willow? Any last words you'd like to leave them with?"

Chelsea's body was shaking in tandem with the victim's. She tried to squeeze her eyes shut, unable to watch another passenger killed.

"Put that gun away, young man."

Chelsea recognized the strong, bold voice even before the old woman stood up in her seat and stepped in front of Willow.

"Put that gun away," Grandma Lucy repeated.

"And why should I?" Bradley snarled.

"Because," the old woman answered boldly, "if you're going to kill anyone, it should be somebody who has lived a full and vibrant life and who is ready to meet her Maker."

Bradley stared at the tiny old woman and scoffed. "You must be out of your mind."

Grandma Lucy shook her head. She barely reached up to Bradley's chest, and yet it somehow looked like she was the one staring down at him.

"I'm not out of my mind," she stated. Her voice was so calm and fearless that Chelsea found herself straining to hear better, as if the old woman's words themselves could give courage to Chelsea's soul.

Grandma Lucy was standing between the young woman and her assailant. Willow took a few steps back until it was just Bradley and Grandma Lucy staring at one another in the aisle.

Bradley had his gun aimed at Grandma Lucy's head. "You must be crazy," he snarled. "Either that or you've got some kind of a death wish."

Chelsea squinted, preparing to shut her eyes in case Bradley shot the old woman right there.

Grandma Lucy's voice didn't falter. "It's not a wish to die per se," she told him, her eyes never leaving his. "But if you shoot me, I know that the moment my soul leaves this frail, old body that I'll find myself in the presence of the Lord, where I'll go on to worship Him eternally. In all honesty, I can't think of a better way to end my life than to save this innocent girl here." She gestured toward Willow, who was hugging her knees and shaking in her seat.

Bradley stared at Grandma Lucy in bewilderment. In the silence, Chelsea could hear the pounding of her heart. For a split second, she was almost convinced that the old woman's faithful conviction would change the hijacker's mind. Chelsea held her breath. Was he going to lower that gun?

Chelsea cast a furtive glance around the cabin. While Bradley was distracted, mesmerized by the spiritual force emanating from this little old lady, it was the perfect time for the other passengers to act. There were hundreds of them and only a few of the terrorists. If the passengers found a way to coordinate their efforts, they could regain control of the plane in a matter of minutes. But how many bullets did Bradley have left in that gun, and how many more lives would be lost in the effort?

Chelsea had been a too young to understand the terrorist attacks of 9/11, but years later, she learned the story about the brave men and women who took down the plane heading for the White House. As far as Chelsea knew, Bradley and his men had no desire to crash their flight at all, but she imagined how much courage and determination it must have taken for the passengers on Flight 93 to do what they did. For the first time, she found herself wondering if everyone on board that day had agreed to the plan, or if some would have preferred to take their chances with the terrorists.

Bradley's apparent moment of wavering passed, and Chelsea watched in horror as he set his jaw and took a step closer to Grandma Lucy. He pressed his gun against her forehead. "Let's see if this God you worship is powerful enough to stop me."

Chelsea scrunched down in her seat, trying to make herself as tiny as she could, her hands ready to cover her ears at the sound of a gunshot that never came.

Bradley stared at his weapon and cursed.

"The gun's jammed," someone shouted. At this declaration, the fear that had paralyzed every single passenger on Flight 219 dissipated in an instant. Several travelers jumped out of their seats, rushing Bradley and his assistant in the Hawaiian shirt.

"We've got them," a man announced victoriously.

It all happened so quickly Chelsea hardly noticed that she had unbuckled her own seat belt and jumped into the aisle. The other passengers had Bradley subdued before Chelsea could do anything to intervene, and she felt somewhat embarrassed for thinking that with her tiny stature she could have done much of anything to help. Still, the passengers had won. The terrorists were caught and bound. The air marshal was awake now and trying to keep the passengers and criminals under control.

Everything was going to be okay.

"Well, folks." The captain's voice over the PA system was comforting and familiar. "It looks like the danger has passed, and we'll be landing in Detroit in just a few minutes. Emergency personnel are already standing by, so once we land, let's let them get on board to do their jobs as quickly as possible. I'd like to thank all of you for remaining calm in a very frightening situation," he concluded, "and lastly, I'd like to thank God who allowed us to arrive in Detroit safe."

Bradley had been dragged to the back of the plane, where two passengers and a flight attendant guarded him with the gun.

"Safe?" he spat, his voice carrying throughout the cabin. "You don't know anything. You're all about to die."

TWELVE

ONCE THEIR PLANE LANDED, it was nearly impossible for Chelsea to recall the exact order of events. Weeks later, as she sat at her favorite café, trying to type out a single sentence to describe what she went through, she couldn't even write one word.

There were those few minutes of relief. The sense that the worst was behind them.

Then Bradley's dire warnings ringing and echoing throughout the cabin as he promised they were all about to die.

At the time, Chelsea attributed his words to the ravings of a madman.

That was before she smelled the smoke.

After the ordeal, Clark told her it was understandable why she couldn't stand the fireworks on New Year's Eve that year. Why even the little poppers her nephew threw on the sidewalk made her cringe.

Chelsea was scarred. That much was for sure. Weeks after that emergency landing at the Detroit airport, she was still having nightmares. Nightmares about smoke and fire alarms. Nightmares about watching innocent people shot in front of her.

In most of her dreams, Bradley was pointing the gun at her, and it was Grandma Lucy who stood between Chelsea and her would-be murderer. After they landed in Detroit, while EMTs rushed to attend to the injured passengers and men in SWAT suits swarmed to arrest Bradley's men, Chelsea had searched for Grandma Lucy in the ensuing chaos.

The old woman was never found.

"Maybe you could ask Google to find her," Mom suggested.

But Chelsea never did.

She talked about Grandma Lucy so much during her coaching calls with Clark that she was sometimes self-conscious.

"She obviously made a big impact on you," Clark told her gently when Chelsea expressed her embarrassment. "There's nothing strange or weird about that. It could be that this little old lady you met saved not only that young woman but the rest of you as well. Who knows how far Bradley would have gone if she hadn't stood up to him?"

Chelsea didn't like to think about all the other what ifs. She was trying hard to move on. She'd written her article on the Brown Elementary School scandal. It wasn't her best work, not by a longshot, but her editor went easy on her after all the trauma she'd gone through.

Clark was willing to bump her up to three coaching sessions a week, stating that an anonymous donor was footing the bill. In all honesty, Chelsea thought he was just gifting his time to her.

She wasn't going to complain.

In the aftermath of the hijacking, Chelsea had made it a point to start going to church more regularly with her parents. When she wasn't spending Sunday mornings with them, she'd visit the church where Brie worked, and they'd go out for lunch afterward. Out of everybody she knew, Brie was the one who seemed the most comfortable letting Chelsea absorb the terror and fear she'd experienced in her own time and in her own way. They talked about Flight 219 every so often. Chelsea found herself particularly upset about the flight attendant who was killed, especially after news stories came out about the two little kids she'd left behind. Sometimes Chelsea felt guilty, as if there was something she could have done to help the passengers who never made it off Flight 219.

But other times, she enjoyed sitting across the café table from her best friend, laughing about a silly Facebook meme or retelling a joke Brie's pastor shared that morning in his sermon.

There were days when Chelsea felt like her despair was getting the best of her, but she was learning to accept that even if she did have lots to be thankful for, there was no shame in feeling down. If anything, Chelsea would have thought that her near-death experience would give her a deeper appreciation for living, but that wasn't always the case. The same inexplicable sense of sadness still impacted her. Not all the time, but enough that she was thankful for the extra sessions with her life coach, thankful for the new antidepressants her mom had encouraged her to talk to the doctor about.

The trauma Chelsea experienced on

board Flight 219 would be enough to fill up a hundred therapy sessions, and even the strongest drugs in the world might not take all the fear completely away. But Chelsea was excited to start a new chapter in her life, a chapter where she learned to accept herself exactly where she was instead of always wishing to be something different or someone else.

A chapter where she appreciated her friends and family and recognized how blessed she was to be surrounded by such an inspiring and encouraging support system.

A chapter where her soul could experience God's love in the midst of trials, joy in the midst of terror, and peace and happiness regardless of her circumstances.

Ms. Rosalie Toth
21-23 Exchange St. Apt. 8F
Binghamton, NY 13901-3813

MN

CPSIA information can be obtained
at www.ICGtesting.com
Printed in the USA
LVHW030956240420
654378LV00004B/1400